CENTRAL ✓ P9-DZA-969

CLASSIC STARTS™

The Three
Musketeers

*Retold from the Alexandre Dumas original
by Oliver Ho*

Illustrated by Jamel Akib

Sterling Publishing Co., Inc.
New York

Library of Congress Cataloging-in-Publication Data

Ho, Oliver.
 The three musketeers / retold from the Alexandre Dumas original by
Oliver Ho ; illustrated by Jamel Akib ; afterword by Arthur Pober.
   p. cm.—(Classic starts)
 Summary: An abridged version of an adventure in seventeenth-century France,
when young d'Artagnan initially quarrels with, then befriends,
three musketeers and joins them in trying to outwit the enemies of the
king and queen.
 ISBN-13: 978-1-4027-3695-7 (alk. paper)
 ISBN-10: 1-4027-3695-9 (alk. paper)
 1. France—History—Louis XIII, 1610–1643—Juvenile fiction. [1. France—History—
Louis XIII, 1610–1643—Fiction. 2. Adventure and adventurers—Fiction.] I. Akib,
Jamel, ill. II. Pober, Arthur. III. Dumas, Alexandre, 1802–1870. Trois mousquetaires.
English. IV. Title. V. Series.

PZ7.H63337Thr 2007
[Fic]—dc22

2006014572

2 4 6 8 10 9 7 5 3 1

Published by Sterling Publishing Co., Inc.
387 Park Avenue South, New York, NY 10016
Copyright © 2007 by Oliver Ho
Illustrations copyright © 2007 by Jamel Akib
c/o Canadian Manda Group, 165 Dufferin Street
Toronto, Ontario, Canada M6K 3H6
Distributed in the United Kingdom by GMC Distribution Services,
Castle Place, 166 High Street, Lewes, East Sussex, England BN7 1XU
Distributed in Australia by Capricorn Link (Australia) Pty. Ltd.
P.O. Box 704, Windsor, NSW 2756, Australia

Classic Starts is a trademark of Sterling Publishing Co., Inc.

Printed in China
All rights reserved

Sterling ISBN-13: 978-1-4027-3695-7
ISBN-10: 1-4027-3695-9

For information about custom editions, special sales, premium and
corporate purchases, please contact Sterling Special Sales
Department at 800-805-5489 or specialsales@sterlingpub.com.

CONTENTS

ↄ

CHAPTER 1

An Adventure in Meung

The town of Meung was used to disturbances of one sort or another, but on that first Monday in April 1625, there seemed to be something special happening. People were shouting and running toward an inn called the Jolly Miller, where a large crowd was watching a young man named D'Artagnan.

A few days earlier, D'Artagnan's father had sent him on a journey to find fortune, adventure, and honor. He had also given his son a letter that would introduce him to Monsieur de Tréville, the leader of the Musketeers.

D'Artagnan was just eighteen years old. He was wearing a faded blue cloak and a little hat with a feather tucked into it. His face was long, thin, and tanned, with high cheekbones and a wide jaw. Too tall to be a child, but too short to be an adult, he looked like a farmer's son on a long journey. Only the large sword hanging from his belt distinguished him as a fighter.

It was D'Artagnan's old yellow horse that had created the sensation. It walked strangely and looked even stranger. As he tied his horse to a post outside the Jolly Miller, D'Artagnan saw a man inside who seemed to be about forty-five years old, with pale skin, piercing black eyes, a black moustache, and a scar across his cheek. He and some men were laughing at D'Artagnan.

Tired of being embarrassed, D'Artagnan chal-lenged the man to a duel. They drew swords, but then the man's friends attacked. D'Artagnan fought them all until someone hit him from behind and knocked him unconscious.

When D'Artagnan awoke, he found that the innkeeper had taken him upstairs. Through the window, he saw the stranger again. He was speaking to a young woman in a horse-drawn carriage. She seemed to be around twenty-five years old, and she was beautiful. The man handed her a box. Through the open window, D'Artagnan heard

him tell the woman to take the box to London on orders from the Cardinal. Then he heard the man call her Milady.

3

The man left before D'Artagnan could catch up with him to finish their duel. Upset and injured, D'Artagnan returned to the inn and stayed for several days. He spent most of his money paying for his stay. When he finally looked for the letter that would introduce him to Monsieur de Tréville, it was gone!

The innkeeper told D'Artagnan that it had fallen from his pocket when he had been knocked out. The man with the scar had seen the letter and seemed very interested in it.

"That scoundrel stole my letter," D'Artagnan said. "I swear I'll find him."

∽

D'Artagnan left the inn and made his way to Paris. When he arrived at Monsieur de Tréville's mansion, he saw many Musketeers practicing with swords, and heard them talking about the

Cardinal and his guards. Although the King ruled France, everyone knew that the Cardinal wanted to take power. Cardinal Richelieu led the church. He had his own soldiers, the Cardinal's Guards, who often fought with the Musketeers.

On the stairs, D'Artagnan passed a tall Musketeer dressed in a sky-blue shirt and a long crimson cloak. Across his chest hung a magnificent golden sash called a baldric. This was not the regular uniform, and the other Musketeers were teasing him about it. D'Artagnan learned that the man's name was Porthos.

"My dear Aramis, make up your mind," Porthos said to another Musketeer. "Are you to be a priest or a Musketeer? Be one or the other, but not both."

"Porthos," Aramis replied, sounding angry, "you are a vain man. Look at your sash. It's far too fancy for a Musketeer. As for me, if I choose to become a priest, then I shall. Meanwhile, I am a Musketeer and I will say what I like. And at this moment, I'm happy to say that I find you a great bore."

Just as D'Artagnan was beginning to wonder why the two men were so angry, the door to Monsieur de Tréville's office opened and he was called inside.

Before D'Artagnan could get very far, Monsieur de Tréville motioned for him to wait, and then shouted three names toward the hallway. At each name, his volume and anger rose.

"Athos! Porthos! Aramis!"

The two men D'Artagnan had seen arguing entered the room. Monsieur de Tréville told them he had learned from the King that several of the Cardinal's guards had fought and defeated them the previous night.

"Tell me, Aramis," said Monsieur de Tréville,

"why did you ask me for a Musketeer's uniform when a priest's frock would have suited you better? And Porthos, what use is such a fancy sash when all it holds up is a sword made of straw? And Athos? Where is Athos?"

The two Musketeers said that Athos was ill, but it was clear that Monsieur de Tréville did not believe them.

"It seems the guardsmen are better soldiers, after all," continued Monsieur de Tréville. "Perhaps I should resign here and apply to be a Lieutenant with them!"

Unable to remain silent anymore, Porthos spoke. He told Monsieur de Tréville that the guards had attacked them first and without warning. Before they could even draw their swords, two Musketeers had been hurt and unable to fight. The fight remained six guards against four Musketeers until Athos was badly hurt. They continued to fight anyway, but the guards overwhelmed them. Luckily, the Musketeers managed to escape.

"I didn't hear about this," said Monsieur de Tréville. "The guards should not have fought unfairly."

Just then, Athos entered. It was clear from his movements that he was still hurt. Monsieur de Tréville tried to shake his hand, but Athos collapsed. A doctor came and took him to another room to recover.

When word arrived back that Athos had woken up and that his wounds would heal, Monsieur de Tréville apologized to the other Musketeers and told them to go. Then he turned his attention back to D'Artagnan.

"I know your father," said Monsieur de Tréville. "He has always been very dear to me. What can I do for his son?"

D'Artagnan asked to become a Musketeer. Monsieur de Tréville told him that he must first prove himself in battle. He offered to have D'Artagnan enrolled in the military academy, where he would learn to be a soldier.

"Alas, Monsieur," said D'Artagnan, "my father gave me a letter for you. I believe it would have convinced you to allow me into the Musketeers. How I wish I had it now."

D'Artagnan told Monsieur de Tréville of his adventure in Meung and the lost letter.

"Your letter had my name written on it?" asked Monsieur de Tréville.

D'Artagnan said it did. After thinking for a few moments, Monsieur de Tréville asked, "Was the man tall with black hair and a moustache? Did he have a scar on his cheek?"

"That's him," said D'Artagnan. "If I ever find him again—"

"He was speaking to a lady?" Monsieur de Tréville interrupted.

D'Artagnan told him of Milady and the

instruction he had overheard—that she was to bring a box to London. Suddenly D'Artagnan looked out the window and shouted, "I see him! The man from Meung—he'll not escape me this time!"

Before Monsieur de Tréville could stop him, D'Artagnan ran from the room.

"Thief!" D'Artagnan shouted. "Coward!"

CHAPTER 2

A Day for Dueling

D'Artagnan raced down the stairs and collided with a Musketeer, who cried out in pain.

"Excuse me," said D'Artagnan. "I'm very sorry, but I'm in a hurry."

He had barely taken a step when someone grabbed his belt and he was pulled backward.

"You're sorry, eh?" said the Musketeer. "You heard how Monsieur de Tréville spoke to my friends and now you think anyone can treat us like that?"

D'Artagnan recognized the Musketeer as

Athos. He tried to apologize again, but Athos was in a bad mood and would not accept. D'Artagnan had no patience for this kind of behavior, even from a Musketeer as brave as Athos. Before he knew it, he had challenged Athos to a duel. The men agreed to fight at noon.

Outside, D'Artagnan saw Porthos speaking to another man in front of the main gate. There was just enough room to run behind Porthos. As he did, a gust of wind blew Porthos's cloak up and D'Artagnan became wrapped in it. Porthos pulled his cloak together and found himself nose-to-nose with D'Artagnan.

"Excuse me," D'Artagnan said, moving out from under the large man's arm. "I am in a great hurry. I was chasing—"

"And you always run blind, I suppose?" Porthos towered over him.

"No, I do not," D'Artagnan said, his temper rising again.

"Do you think you can just push past me?" Porthos asked. "You should have asked before barging through."

"I was in a hurry," D'Artagnan said. "This is very important. And you are also very large and your cloak is too long. It was in my way——"

"What?" Porthos shouted.

The two men argued and, as quickly as it had happened with Athos, D'Artagnan found himself agreeing to another duel. This one was set for one o'clock in the same place where D'Artagnan was to fight Athos.

D'Artagnan resumed his chase, but the man from Meung was gone. Suddenly the events of the morning began to sink in. D'Artagnan had disgraced himself in front of Monsieur de Tréville by rushing out like that. Then he had challenged two dangerous men to duels. What's worse, he thought of those two men as heroes!

What a fool I am, D'Artagnan thought. *I should*

try to be like Aramis. Didn't he seem friendly and graceful?

Suddenly D'Artagnan saw Aramis talking with some other men. This time, D'Artagnan decided to be careful and polite. He saw a handkerchief under Aramis's boot and picked it up.

"Here, Monsieur," D'Artagnan said. "I believe you dropped this."

Aramis snatched it quickly and the other men began to tease him.

"So, Aramis," one of them said, "if you truly don't know Madame de Bois-Tracy, why do you have her handkerchief?"

"You are mistaken," Aramis said. "This does not belong to me. Perhaps it fell from your pocket."

"I'm sorry," D'Artagnan said, trying to help. "I didn't see it fall from anyone's pocket. I just saw it under your shoe."

The men left, still laughing at Aramis, who walked in the other direction. D'Artagnan ran after him to apologize. Unfortunately, Aramis was now embarrassed and angry. Instead of accepting the apology, he called D'Artagnan a fool for his behavior. Once again, D'Artagnan lost his temper. He quickly challenged Aramis to a duel, and they agreed to meet at two o'clock.

I don't think I'll survive this, D'Artagnan thought. *Well, if I am to be killed, at least I'll be killed by a Musketeer.*

D'Artagnan was convinced that he couldn't win three duels, but he wasn't the sort of person to just give up. Instead, he thought about how he could outsmart the three Musketeers. Soon he arrived at the meeting place for his duel with Athos: a small monastery surrounded by empty fields.

Athos was waiting with his typical calm and dignity. From his movements, it was clear that he was still injured.

"Monsieur, I have asked two friends to be with

me today," Athos told D'Artagnan. "They should be here soon. I don't know why they're late."

"I have no one to be here with me," D'Artagnan said. "The only person I know in this city is Monsieur de Tréville."

After a moment's thought, Athos said, "He's your only friend? Well look here, if I kill you, I shall be taken for an ogre. You are far too young for this."

"No one will say you overpowered me," D'Artagnan said. "After all, your wounds still seem to be giving you trouble."

"They are very troublesome, indeed," Athos said. "You hurt me when you ran into me. But I can fight just as well with my other hand."

"If you would allow me to make an offer," D'Artagnan said, "my mother gave me some medicine that works well for curing wounds. You can have some. I'm sure you will be healed in a few days. We can duel then if you like."

Suddenly the men saw Porthos and Aramis approaching.

"Finally, my friends have arrived," Athos said.

"You asked *them* to be here?" D'Artagnan asked.

"Of course," Athos replied. "We are best friends."

Porthos and Aramis asked D'Artagnan why he was there so soon. The Musketeers were confused when they discovered that they were all to duel with him.

"Athos, why are you fighting with him?" Aramis asked.

"Actually, I'm not sure. He accidentally hurt my shoulder," Athos said. "What about you, Porthos?"

"I'm fighting," Porthos began. Then he blushed. "I'm fighting because I'm fighting!"

D'Artagnan smiled and said, "We had a slight disagreement over fashion."

"And you, Aramis?" asked Athos.

"Oh, ours is a religious quarrel," Aramis said, and made a sign to D'Artagnan that they should keep the real reason a secret.

"Now that you are all here," D'Artagnan said, "allow me to offer my apologies. Do not misunderstand me. I apologize only that I can't settle my score with all of you. Monsieur Athos has the first right to kill me, which lessens the value of your claim, Monsieur Porthos, and makes yours, Monsieur Aramis, practically worthless. So I repeat, gentlemen, please excuse me—but on that score alone. Come, on guard!"

D'Artagnan bowed and drew his sword. But just as he and Athos were about to begin, a group of the Cardinal's guards arrived and accused the Musketeers of dueling. Then they tried to arrest all four men.

"There are five of them and only three of us," Athos said to his friends. "If we are taken in, I would not be able to face Monsieur de Tréville. I would rather take my chances here."

"Allow me to correct you," D'Artagnan said. "There are four of us. I don't wear a Musketeer's uniform, but my heart is that of a Musketeer."

"What is your name, my brave fellow?" Athos asked.

"D'Artagnan, Monsieur."

"Well then," Athos cried, "Athos, Porthos, Aramis, and D'Artagnan, forward!"

D'Artagnan fought with the leader of the guards, who made the mistake of thinking him too young to know how to use a sword. After a short fight, D'Artagnan easily defeated him and left him with an injury to the leg.

Then D'Artagnan looked over the field. Only Athos seemed to be losing strength, so D'Artagnan ran to his aid and disarmed his opponent. At the same time, Aramis disarmed his man. The leader of the guards realized that his men had lost and ordered the last soldier to stop fighting with Porthos.

The Musketeers took the guards' swords as trophies and left the field arm-in-arm with D'Artagnan. As they walked, every Musketeer they met joined them until there was a victory parade marching toward Monsieur de Tréville's mansion.

The fight caused a scandal. In public, Monsieur de Tréville scolded the men, but in private he congratulated them. Soon after, he told the King how D'Artagnan had fought at the Musketeers' side and helped them win.

"A brave lad," the King said, pleased that his soldiers had proven to be better than the Cardinal's.

The King congratulated the Musketeers. He singled out D'Artagnan for his youth and bravery and gave him several gold coins. Then the King whispered to Monsieur de Tréville, "I know every

Musketeer must first have a trial period as a soldier. Let's put this lad in service as one of the Cardinal's guards. It will be good to have a trustworthy man there."

Monsieur de Tréville went to tell D'Artagnan and found the young man dividing his prize evenly with the three Musketeers.

CHAPTER 3

A New Adventure for
New Friends

 ⟨ᴑ⟩

D'Artagnan asked his new friends how he should spend the King's money. Porthos suggested he hire a helper, and even brought a suitable candidate by that night—a young man named Planchet. He needed work and took the job as D'Artagnan's assistant.

Each Musketeer had someone to help him. Athos had Grimaud, Porthos had Mousqueton, and Aramis had Bazin.

Athos was barely thirty years old, handsome, and smart. Grimaud had served him for several years and the two men rarely spoke. Athos could make a small gesture and Grimaud would act.

Porthos was almost the opposite of Athos. Not only did he talk a lot, but he talked loudly and enjoyed the sound of his own voice. Porthos knew he wasn't as smart or graceful as Athos. Instead, he drew attention to himself by buying the most expensive things. He even dressed Mousqueton in his old (but still fancy) clothes.

As for Aramis, he had trained to be a priest before becoming a Musketeer. His assistant, Bazin, wished Aramis would return to his old life. He would much rather be an assistant to a priest than to a Musketeer.

D'Artagnan and the three Musketeers quickly became best friends. When they finally used up the King's money, the four men took turns buying dinners and looking after one another.

D'Artagnan wanted to do more to help his friends. One day while he was thinking of a plan, he heard a light knock on his door. Planchet let in D'Artagnan's landlord, a man named Bonacieux.

"I heard you are a courageous young man," said Monsieur Bonacieux. "If that is true, I have a secret I must share. Perhaps you can help me."

"Speak, Monsieur, speak," said D'Artagnan, sensing that this could be the adventure he was looking for.

"My wife is a seamstress for the Queen," Monsieur Bonacieux began nervously. "She is very beautiful."

"And?"

"And she was kidnapped yesterday!" Monsieur Bonacieux said. "It happened as she was leaving her workroom. I don't know who did it, but I suspect a strange man who has been following her for some time. I think it has to do with politics— some intrigue between the Queen and another

25

man. The Queen trusts my wife, you see, and tells her many secrets that she wouldn't tell anyone else. My wife sees the Queen every day and they have become quite close. I'm afraid my wife may have been trying to help Her Majesty."

Monsieur Bonacieux told D'Artagnan that the Queen was secretly in love with a man from England named the Duke of Buckingham. The Cardinal was trying to embarrass the King by revealing the Queen's secret. The Queen had recently learned that someone pretending to be her had contacted the Duke and asked him to come to France. This was the Cardinal's plan to expose her secret. Monsieur Bonacieux was sure that his wife had been kidnapped so that the Cardinal could learn more about the Queen's plans.

"Tell me about the stranger who was following your wife," D'Artagnan said.

"He's a nobleman of lofty bearing. He has

black hair, eyes that pierce, and a scar on his cheek."

"A scar," said D'Artagnan. "Why, that's my man of Meung!"

"So you know him?" asked Monsieur Bonacieux, handing over a piece of paper. "I believe he sent me this."

"Do not look for your wife," D'Artagnan read. "She will be returned when she is no longer needed. If you try to find her, she will be lost to you forever."

"I have seen you surrounded by Musketeers," said Monsieur Bonacieux. "Naturally, I thought you and your friends would be delighted to help the Queen and ruin the Cardinal's plans. If you help me, I will forgive the three months' rent you still owe. In fact, you will never need to pay me rent again. I could even lend you any money you need."

"That would be very helpful, indeed," said D'Artagnan.

"He's there!" Monsieur Bonacieux interrupted, standing and pointing out D'Artagnan's window. "It's the man who kidnapped my wife!"

D'Artagnan looked out of the window and saw the man from Meung.

"This time he will not escape me!" D'Artagnan said.

On the way down the stairs he met Athos, Porthos, and Aramis, who were coming up to meet him.

"The man from Meung!" D'Artagnan yelled and ran past them.

CHAPTER 4

D'Artagnan Finds
Madame Bonacieux

Athos, Porthos, and Aramis continued the climb to D'Artagnan's apartment. They had seen him chase after the mysterious man before and knew he would return soon.

"He vanished like a phantom," D'Artagnan said when he came back. "His flight may have cost us all a lot of money."

He told his friends Monsieur Bonacieux's story and explained that Madame Bonacieux's kidnapper and the man from Meung were the same person.

"You're in luck," Athos said. "Your landlord is wealthy enough to pay us for this adventure. The only question is whether the money is worth risking our lives."

"You forget about the victim," D'Artagnan said. "The poor woman was kidnapped because she was trying to help her Queen. I believe the Cardinal is behind this. As an enemy of the Queen, he is our enemy, too, my friends. If we could find some way to ruin his plans, I would gladly risk my life."

"According to your landlord's tale, the Queen believes that the Duke has come to Paris to meet her, but the letter inviting him was fake?" Athos asked.

"Indeed," said D'Artagnan. "We must find a way to warn the Duke and save Madame Bonacieux."

Suddenly the men heard footsteps rushing up the stairs. The door flew open and in came Monsieur Bonacieux.

"Save me, gentlemen," he cried.

At that moment, four of the Cardinal's guards arrived. When they saw the other men, they began to look nervous, but D'Artagnan invited the guards in. They said they had come to arrest Monsieur Bonacieux, and D'Artagnan told them to go ahead. To Monsieur Bonacieux, he whispered, "We can only save you by remaining free. If we fight these men, we will be arrested, too."

The guards took Monsieur Bonacieux away. He was confused and scared, but he agreed to trust D'Artagnan.

When the Musketeers were alone, D'Artagnan said, "And now gentlemen, all for one and one for all. That is our motto, is it not?"

"That is correct. Your swords, my friends," Athos said.

The four men held their swords together and as one they repeated the words.

"All for one and one for all!"

"Excellent," D'Artagnan said. "Remember, from now on we are at war with the Cardinal."

The men parted ways to look into Madame Bonacieux's disappearance, to look for the man from Meung, and to try to learn more about the plot to catch the Duke of Buckingham. D'Artagnan stayed at home. He watched Monsieur Bonacieux's apartment, which was directly below his, through a hole in his floor.

Soon he saw some men dressed in black enter the apartment downstairs. Later that night, someone else entered the apartment and D'Artagnan heard the men attack. Then he heard cries and a moan—a woman's voice.

"I live here, I tell you," the woman said. "I am Madame Bonacieux! I work for the Queen."

"You are exactly the person we've been waiting for," said one of the men.

D'Artagnan told Planchet to get the other Musketeers. Then he raced downstairs and knocked on the door to the apartment below. When the door opened, he rushed inside.

The whole neighborhood heard loud cries, stamping feet, a clash of swords, and the smashing of many pieces of furniture. Then the door opened and the four men in black ran out, their clothes in tatters.

Alone with Madame Bonacieux, D'Artagnan saw that she was about twenty-five years old, with dark hair and blue eyes. She thanked him and asked why those men had tried to rob her.

"Madame, those men were more dangerous than thieves," D'Artagnan said. "They were agents of the Cardinal. His guards arrested your husband earlier today. Monsieur Bonacieux hired my friends and me to find you and the man who took you. How did you escape?"

"I climbed through the window of the room where they were keeping me," she said. "Oh, what shall I do?"

"We can't stay here," D'Artagnan said. "I've sent for my friends, but I don't know when they will arrive. More guards could come at any moment. Follow me."

D'Artagnan took her to Athos's home. The Musketeer was gone, but D'Artagnan had a key. Once inside, Madame Bonacieux told D'Artagnan to go to the palace and tell one of her friends where she was.

D'Artagnan followed her instructions. Later, walking on his own, he realized he had begun to fall in love with her. To an apprentice Musketeer, she represented the ideal of love. She was beautiful and mysterious, and she knew many secrets of the Court. But there was more to it. He wanted to be a hero for her. He felt foolish and decided to ask Aramis for his advice.

Aramis probably ran to my apartment when Planchet called on him, D'Artagnan thought. *He must be home by now.*

When D'Artagnan arrived at his friend's house, he saw someone crouching in the shadows. He was afraid that one of the Cardinal's agents was after his friend. The figure in the shadows went to the front door and D'Artagnan realized it was a woman. She passed under the street lamp and he saw that it was Madame Bonacieux!

CHAPTER 5

A Mysterious Night

The door opened and Madame Bonacieux spoke to a young woman inside. D'Artagnan watched as they exchanged handkerchiefs.

What does this mean? he wondered.

When Madame Bonacieux left and hurried down the street, D'Artagnan ran after her. He touched her shoulder and she cried out.

"It's you!" she said. "Oh, thank goodness. Why have you followed me?"

"I was about to visit my friend. He lives in that house. Do you know Aramis?"

"I don't," she said. "I was talking to a woman."

"Who is she?"

"That is a secret," she said. "If you still want to help me, please walk with me to my next meeting. Once we arrive, you must go."

D'Artagnan did not want to leave her, especially with so many guards and secrets flying about. But when they arrived at her destination, he agreed to go home. Back at his apartment, Planchet told D'Artagnan that he had only been able to bring Athos back. But some more guards had come and arrested him!

"They thought he was you," Planchet said. "He told me, 'D'Artagnan needs his freedom right now. The police will think they have him, which should give him a few days.'"

"Brave Athos," D'Artagnan said. "I must find Monsieur de Tréville and tell him what has happened. Will you stay here? You're not afraid?"

"Don't worry," Planchet said. "I can be brave when I put my mind to it."

On his way to Monsieur de Tréville's mansion, D'Artagnan saw a man and woman walking together. The man wore a Musketeer's uniform. D'Artagnan thought he looked like Aramis, so he ran to them. The man turned, but it wasn't Aramis. The woman turned as well. It was Madame Bonacieux again!

"I had your promise," she said. "You swore you wouldn't follow me."

"I'm sorry. I thought this man was someone else," D'Artagnan said.

"Please take my arm, Madame," the man said. "Let us go on."

D'Artagnan was confused and wouldn't move out of their way, so the man stepped forward and pushed him aside. D'Artagnan and the man both drew their swords.

"My Lord, don't fight!" Madame Bonacieux said.

"My Lord?" D'Artagnan said. "Can you possibly be—"

"It's the Duke of Buckingham," Madame Bonacieux said. "And now you may have ruined us all!"

"Please forgive me," D'Artagnan said. "I only wanted to protect her."

"You are a worthy young man," said the Duke. "If you wish to help, follow us at a distance. If you see anyone else following us, attack them."

D'Artagnan followed behind Madame Bonacieux and the Duke until they entered the Palace. Inside, Madame Bonacieux led the Duke through many dark and secret passages. Finally they reached one of the Queen's rooms.

When the Queen entered, the Duke was struck by her beauty. She was twenty-six, with eyes that sparkled like emeralds. The Duke kneeled at her feet.

"My Lord Duke," the Queen said. "You must already know that I did not invite you here."

"I know," he said. "But I am in love with you and I wanted to see you again."

"You must listen to me," she said. "Our kingdoms separate us. We must never meet again. Remember, I never told you that I loved you."

"But you never said that you didn't love me," he said.

It was true that she loved him, but it was too dangerous. If the King found out, the Duke's life would be in danger and the scandal could lead to a war with England. Just then, as if reading her thoughts, the Duke told her he wanted their kingdoms to go to war.

"A war ends in peace," he explained. "And peace requires an ambassador such as myself to come back to France and sign the papers. Then I shall see you again and no one will be able to stop me."

"You are a foolish man," the Queen said. "You must go now. I don't want to see you harmed."

"Madame, let me beg for an object from you, something to prove that I'm not dreaming," said the Duke.

"Will you leave France and return to England?" the Queen asked.

"I swear it."

She went into her room, and returned with a small wooden jewelry box.

"My Lord, here is a gift for you to remember me by," the Queen said.

The Duke fell to one knee.

"You promised to leave," the Queen reminded him.

"I shall be true to my word, Your Highness,"

the Duke said. "Just give me your hand, and I'll go."

Her eyes closed, the Queen offered him one hand, and leaned with the other on the table, for she felt as if she was about to faint. Passionately, the Duke pressed his lips to her fingertips, then rose and left the room.

෨

While all this was happening, Monsieur Bonacieux sat in a small room at the jail. He was very scared. His cowardice was so strong, in fact, that it outweighed any love he had for his wife. He would have revealed all of her secrets if only they would free him. But when the guards asked him where they could find Madame Bonacieux, he could only tell them that she had been kidnapped.

"She escaped yesterday afternoon," said a

guard. "Thanks to your efforts and those of Monsieur D'Artagnan. Luckily for you, we have arrested him as well."

The guards opened the door and brought in Athos.

"Monsieur D'Artagnan, will you explain what you and Monsieur Bonacieux have planned?" the guard asked.

"But that is not D'Artagnan," said Monsieur Bonacieux.

"Not D'Artagnan! Then who is this man?" the guard asked.

"I can't tell you," said Monsieur Bonacieux. "I don't know him."

"Your name, Monsieur," snapped the guard.

"My name is Athos."

"But you said your name was D'Artagnan," the guard said.

"No, Monsieur. When the guards came, one of them asked if I was Monsieur D'Artagnan. I said, 'Do you really think so?' and the guards said they were positive. Who was I to say they were wrong?"

"Where is my wife?" interrupted Monsieur Bonacieux.

The guard told him that she was in trouble and then sent the men back to their cells. Athos shrugged and left. Monsieur Bonacieux began to shake with fear.

⟡

The next day, the guards took Monsieur Bonacieux to see the Cardinal. The poor man was shocked to be questioned by such a powerful person.

"You have plotted with your wife," the Cardinal said. "Together you helped the Queen meet with the Duke of Buckingham."

"But my wife told me it was you who tricked

the Duke into coming here," said Monsieur Bonacieux.

"Hold your tongue, you fool!" the Cardinal said.

Just then the door opened and the man from Meung entered. Monsieur Bonacieux shouted, "That's the man. That man kidnapped my wife!"

The Cardinal called for his guards.

"Take this man away," he said, and pointed at Monsieur Bonacieux.

The man from Meung—whose real name was Count Rochefort—spoke to the Cardinal.

"The Queen has met with the Duke," he said. "My spies saw him leave the palace last night."

"We have been beaten," the Cardinal said. "Now we must seek revenge."

"I have learned that the Queen gave the Duke a gift," said Rochefort. "A box with some jewelry inside—diamond studs to wear on the shoulder."

"Those diamonds were a gift from the King,"

the Cardinal replied. "Perhaps this is how we shall catch them. We must create a situation where the Queen has to wear the diamonds. When she reveals that she no longer has them, she will be found out. We must make the Queen believe she is safe. She must not suspect that we know about the diamonds."

The Cardinal wrote a short note and told Rochefort to make sure it was delivered to his spy, Milady, in London. The note instructed her to find the Duke and wait for him to wear the diamonds. When he did, Milady was to secretly cut two of them off and bring them to the Cardinal.

When Rochefort left, the Cardinal asked his guards to bring Bonacieux back up.

"I must apologize," the Cardinal told him. "I realize that I was mistaken. You are a worthy man. I hope there are no hard feelings."

Monsieur Bonacieux, who had begun to think that he would be in jail forever, was surprised.

"No hard feelings?" he said, stuttering.

"You are free to go," the Cardinal said. "I hope we shall meet again soon. I enjoy your company very much. In fact, I will have some money sent to you as my apology for putting you in jail."

Monsieur Bonacieux bowed and thanked the Cardinal many times. When he left, the Cardinal thought, *There goes a man who will do anything I ask. He will spy on his wife, and will tell me everything he learns.*

The next day, the Cardinal met with the King.

"Sire, the Duke was in Paris," the Cardinal said. "He left this morning."

"What was he doing here?" the King asked, alarmed.

"My spies tell me he met with the Queen," the Cardinal replied.

The King had suspected for a long time that the Queen was in love with someone else. What he did not know was that the Cardinal had also been in love with the Queen once, many years ago. She had turned him down and the Cardinal had been trying to find ways to hurt her ever since.

"What shall I do?" the King asked. "I must find out what she's plotting."

"I hate to see you and the Queen angry with each other," the Cardinal said. "I think I know a way to solve this."

The Cardinal reminded the King how much the Queen loved fancy parties.

"Perhaps she will be happy if you offer to throw a party for her," the Cardinal said. "It will also give her a chance to wear the diamonds you gave her. She hasn't worn them for some time."

"We shall see," the King said. "It is a good idea."

Just then, a messenger arrived with a letter for the Cardinal. He left the King for a moment to read the letter. It was from Milady. The note said, "I have the diamonds, but I cannot leave London yet. I will need money. I should be back in Paris in two weeks."

The Cardinal smiled to himself. This would be a perfect opportunity to embarrass the King and Queen.

"Sire, I have another idea," the Cardinal said when he returned. "If you offer to have the Queen's party in two weeks, it will give her enough time to plan and to invite everyone. And remember to tell her how beautiful those diamonds will look."

CHAPTER 6

A Letter for London

The King was suspicious. He had been fooled by the Cardinal before and did not wish to be humiliated again.

"I'm eager to see you wearing the diamonds I gave you," the King said when he told the Queen about the party.

The Queen grew nervous when she heard this. The King was watching her closely. He noticed that the subject of the diamonds seemed to upset her.

"When exactly is the party?" she asked.

"I forget the date," the King said. "I will ask the Cardinal."

"So this was the Cardinal's idea?" she asked.

"Certainly. Why do you ask?"

"And was it also his idea that I wear the diamonds?" the Queen asked.

"What does that matter?" the King replied.

"It doesn't," the Queen said.

"Good," said the King. He thought about her reaction and tried to understand what her secret could be. "I shall count on seeing them."

After the King left, the Queen began to cry.

What shall I do? she thought. *The Cardinal must know everything already, and soon the King will know, too.*

Suddenly a voice from behind her asked, "Can I help, your majesty?" It was Madame Bonacieux.

"You have nothing to fear," she said. "You can trust me. Those diamonds were in the box you gave to the Duke, were they not? We must get them back."

"But how?" the Queen asked. "They are with him in London. The King and Cardinal will be watching everyone who tries to travel there."

"Write a letter to the Duke. I will make sure it gets to him," Madame Bonacieux said. "My husband is a good, honest man. He will do anything I ask."

The Queen thanked her and wrote a short note explaining everything to the Duke, which Madame Bonacieux took and ran home. To her surprise, her thoughts kept returning to D'Artagnan. He was brave and handsome, and he seemed to be very much in love with her.

Meanwhile, Monsieur Bonacieux was thinking about the Cardinal's friendliness and dreaming that the Cardinal would make him rich.

"I have something important to tell you," Madame Bonacieux told her husband when she entered their apartment. "You must help me deliver a letter to a man in London. I can't tell you more, but believe me, this is very important."

Monsieur Bonacieux hadn't seen his wife in a week and was angry that she didn't ask about his stay in jail or explain how she had escaped from her kidnappers.

"Don't you want to know what has happened to me?" he asked.

"Yes, of course," she said. "But this business is much more important. Our future may depend on it."

"Our fortunes have changed since I last saw you," he said. "In the past week I have become a close friend of the Cardinal."

He held up a small bag of coins.

"He has been very kind to us. Look at this money he gave me."

"You would serve a man who mistreats your wife and insults your Queen?" asked Madame

Bonacieux, shocked. "You must be careful. The Cardinal's friendship can disappear as quickly as it arrived. We should serve the people greater than him."

"I only serve the Cardinal now. There is no one greater," he said. "What on earth did you want me to do, anyway? What's this letter, and who's in London?"

Madame Bonacieux worried that her husband would ruin her plans.

"Oh, it was nothing," she said, pretending to change her mind. "I just wanted to order some dresses. I thought we might sell them here."

Her husband didn't believe her and decided to report to the Cardinal. He told her he had to run an errand and hurried away.

Left alone, Madame Bonacieux felt helpless.

What have I done? she thought. *I promised to help the Queen, and now my own husband works for her enemy.*

There was a knock on her ceiling. She looked up and heard D'Artagnan's voice.

"Madame, please open the side door. I shall come downstairs at once."

D'Artagnan came in and told her that he had been listening through the floor of his room.

"Your husband is certainly a sorry specimen," he said. "But from your conversation with him I learned four things. First, I learned that he is a fool. Second, I learned that you are in distress, which makes me happy because it gives me a chance to help you. Third, I realized that I would risk anything to help you. And fourth, I learned that the Queen needs someone to go to London on her behalf. That is why I am here."

As Madame Bonacieux looked at D'Artagnan, her last doubt vanished. There was so much love in his eyes and strength in his voice that she had to trust him.

"I can't tell you any more than I told my husband," she said. "I can only say that this letter must be delivered to the address on the envelope, nothing more. Believe me, Her Majesty will not be ungrateful."

"I need no reward," D'Artagnan said. "I love you and that is enough for me."

"Hush!" she whispered. "There is a voice in the street. Do you hear? It's my husband."

D'Artagnan led Madame Bonacieux up to his apartment, where they spied through the floor and saw Monsieur Bonacieux talking to another man—it was the man from Meung!

CHAPTER 7

A Dangerous Journey to London

"I have sworn to kill that man," D'Artagnan said.

"Your life is now devoted to a nobler cause," Madame Bonacieux told him. "I forbid you to face any danger other than your mission for the Queen. Now listen with me. We must hear what they're talking about."

"She wanted me to deliver a letter to London," Monsieur Bonacieux said.

"Did she mention any names?" Count Rochefort asked.

"Unfortunately she did not," said Monsieur Bonacieux. "Do you think the Cardinal will be interested in this news?"

"He would have been happier to see the letter," Rochefort said.

"That may still be possible," said Monsieur Bonacieux. "I'll tell her I wish to help her. She will give me the letter and I will bring it to you."

D'Artagnan stepped away from the hole in the floor. He was excited to have a mission that would bring him glory and money. More important, he knew this mission would prove his love for Madame Bonacieux. But first he had to tell Monsieur de Tréville what he had learned.

"Monsieur, the Queen's honor, perhaps her very life, is at stake," D'Artagnan said when he was admitted to Monsieur de Tréville's office. "I have been told a secret."

"Is it your own secret?" asked Tréville.

"It is the Queen's," D'Artagnan said.

"Then keep it to yourself. Tell me what you wish me to do, but do not reveal Her Majesty's secret, even to me."

"I need two weeks to go to London," D'Artagnan replied.

"Will anyone try to stop you?"

"The Cardinal would give the world to stop me."

"Then you will not survive your journey alone," said Monsieur de Tréville. "Take your friends. I will arrange for all four of you to have two weeks away."

Soon after, D'Artagnan told his friends that they had to leave for London immediately. The four men gathered their horses, called for their assistants, and traveled through the night. They didn't stop until they reached an inn the next morning. They went in for some food and saw several men in the dining room.

One of the men stopped Porthos and told

him they should have a toast to the Cardinal. Porthos agreed, but said he would also like to have a toast to the King. The stranger said he didn't like the King and Porthos called the man a fool. The stranger quickly drew his sword and challenged Porthos to a duel.

"You are foolish," Athos said to Porthos, "but never mind. You can't stop now. Take care of this man and join us afterward."

"Why did that man choose Porthos?" Aramis asked as they rode away.

"Porthos was speaking louder than the rest of us," D'Artagnan said. "That fellow must have thought Porthos was our leader. I hope Porthos defeats him soon and will be able to catch up with us quickly."

Later that day, the men came to a narrow part of the road where workmen were digging and blocking the way. As the Musketeers passed, the workmen suddenly began to throw rocks at them.

"It's an ambush!" D'Artagnan yelled. "We can't waste time here. We must be off!"

The Musketeers rode away, but Aramis's shoulder had been hurt badly in the attack. He rode for a few hours before he finally had to stop.

"I will be fine, my friends," said Aramis. "There is a priest's school near here. I can catch up on my studies while I recover. I will wait for Porthos."

Athos and D'Artagnan continued on with their assistants, leaving Aramis and Bazin behind. After several hours, they stopped at another inn, where they decided to stay until morning. When Athos went to pay, the innkeeper looked at the money and called Athos a counterfeiter.

"What are you talking about?" Athos said. "These coins are real."

Suddenly several men entered by the side door and attacked Athos.

"I'm trapped!" Athos yelled out to the others. "Run, D'Artagnan!"

D'Artagnan and Planchet rode their horses as fast as they could, sad to be the last of the band of travelers.

At last, they arrived at the port of Calais. They went to buy tickets to London, and listened as the man in front of them tried to do the same.

"I would love to sell you a ticket," the ship's captain told the man. "But I received orders that no one is to sail unless they have permission from the Cardinal."

"I have a letter of permission here," said the man. "I must travel to London for my business. I spoke to the Cardinal a few days ago."

"Very good," said the captain. "Go show it to the commissioner, in that building there. After he has stamped it, I can sell you a ticket. We're leaving soon, so hurry up."

D'Artagnan knew he needed that man's letter of permission, so he followed him. Before the man arrived at the commissioner's office, D'Artagnan stopped him and demanded the letter. The man refused, believing D'Artagnan to be a thief. The men fought and D'Artagnan won easily, leaving the man injured. With the man's letter in hand, D'Artagnan went to the commissioner's office, had him stamp it, and bought a ticket to London.

CHAPTER 8

The Queen's Diamonds

∽

D'Artagnan and Planchet arrived in London and hurried to see the Duke of Buckingham. The Duke was impressed that D'Artagnan, who looked so young, had made it all the way to London with someone as powerful as the Cardinal trying to stop him. When he read the Queen's letter, he cried out, "You must come with me at once!"

"The Queen gave these to me," the Duke said, removing the diamonds from the jewelry box. "Now she needs them back. So be it."

The Duke took a closer look at the diamonds.

"Wait! Two are missing. See here, they have been cut away."

"Who could have done that?" D'Artagnan asked.

"I only wore these once," the Duke said. "It was at a party where a woman named Lady Clarik stood beside me for a long time. She must be one of the Cardinal's spies."

The Duke called for a jeweler and ordered him to make replacements for the lost diamonds. By the time the diamonds were complete, there was only one day left before the King's party.

"How will I get back in time?" D'Artagnan asked. "The Cardinal will be watching every ship, and it will take too long to go by land."

"You will go by land," the Duke said. "I have arranged for you to have a fresh horse at every stop along the way. My men will take care of you."

D'Artagnan thanked the Duke and left for Paris. As the Duke had promised, a fresh horse was waiting whenever D'Artagnan stopped. Traveling this way, D'Artagnan rode nonstop and arrived in Paris on the day of the party.

Everyone was talking about the event. The King and the Cardinal were excited, each for their own reasons. Both men wanted to see if the Queen would be wearing the diamonds. The King was worried that his suspicions about the Queen's betrayal were correct. The Cardinal hoped to expose her secret and embarrass the King.

Just before she arrived, the Cardinal showed the King two diamonds.

"These come from the set you gave her," the Cardinal said. "If she is wearing the diamonds when you see her, please ask her how these two could have been stolen."

When the Queen entered the room, the King

and the Cardinal made their way through the crowd to inspect her clothes. She was wearing the diamonds on her shoulder.

"Thank you for wearing my gift," the King said, looking at the diamonds. "But I believe two of them are missing. The Cardinal is waiting to return them to you."

"What's this?" the Queen said, pretending to be surprised. "Are you giving me two more? Mine are all here, as you can see."

The King looked closely.

"So they are," he said, and looked at the Cardinal. "What does this mean, then?"

The Cardinal looked embarrassed.

"It means that I wanted to give the Queen these diamonds myself," he said, stuttering. "Only I was too shy, so I made up this story."

The Queen smiled and thanked both men. The King appeared to be quite happy, but the Cardinal was red with anger.

D'Artagnan watched everything from the side of the room. Suddenly Madame Bonacieux touched him on the shoulder. She led him through the palace to a small room with a curtain, where she told him to wait.

A few minutes later, several people entered the room on the other side of the curtain. From her voice, D'Artagnan recognized the Queen. She reached through the curtain and D'Artagnan touched her hand. As soon as he did, she dropped a large and valuable ring in his palm.

D'Artagnan put the ring on his finger and then hurried home. When he arrived, Planchet told him that a letter had come from Madame Bonacieux—a short note asking him to meet her the next night. D'Artagnan's heart filled with love and he read the note many times. She had signed it. Finally D'Artagnan knew her first name: Constance.

The next morning, Monsieur de Tréville

told D'Artagnan that the King was in a good mood. The Cardinal, on the other hand, was not.

"Obviously your return has something to do with this," said Monsieur de Tréville. "You will have to be very cautious now. The Cardinal will seek revenge. He is not a man to play tricks on."

"Do you think he suspects that I went to London?" D'Artagnan asked.

"Is that where you found the enormous ring you're wearing?" asked Monsieur de Tréville.

"This was a gift from the Queen," D'Artagnan said. "She gave it to me in secret last night."

"Oh my," Monsieur de Tréville said, looking worried. "You must sell that ring as soon as you can."

"I don't see what I have to fear," D'Artagnan said.

"Right now you are as safe as a man sitting on a bomb with a burning fuse," said Monsieur de Tréville. "I could see that ring from across the street. Believe me, the Cardinal has a good memory and a long reach. He will try to seek revenge on you and your friends. Where are they, anyway?"

"I was about to ask if you had heard from them," D'Artagnan said.

He told Monsieur de Tréville of their adventures on the way to London. Monsieur de Tréville listened closely and then told D'Artagnan that it would be safer to leave the city for a few days.

"I will leave tomorrow," D'Artagnan said. "I have an appointment tonight that I cannot miss."

CHAPTER 9

D'Artagnan Loses His Love, but Finds Porthos

∽

D'Artagnan made his way to his meeting with Constance Bonacieux at a small house on the outskirts of the city.

He arrived on time and waited for her outside. After a few hours, he decided to look in a lit window on the second floor. He climbed a tree and was shocked at the sight inside. The room was a mess, as if there had been a great struggle. D'Artagnan began to panic. He was worried that Constance had been kidnapped again.

He ran to a house across the road, where an old man answered the door. D'Artagnan begged the old man to tell him if anything strange had happened at the house across the street.

The man said that five men had kicked open the door of the house and dragged a young woman out. She had been screaming. They carried her to a carriage and drove away.

"Only one of the men didn't wear a sword. He was short and fat, older, nearly bald," the old man said. "The ringleader was a tall man with a mustache and black eyes. I believe he had a scar on his face."

With a heavy heart, D'Artagnan returned home. Monsieur Bonacieux was waiting for someone outside and grew nervous when he saw D'Artagnan. D'Artagnan was suspicious of everyone and studied his landlord closely. Then he thought, *Short and fat, older, nearly bald. Monsieur Bonacieux helped kidnap his own wife!*

D'Artagnan hurried up to his room, where Planchet told him that two messages had arrived earlier. One was a letter for Aramis. The other was for D'Artagnan. The Cardinal wanted to see him immediately.

This is too much, D'Artagnan thought. *Now the Cardinal himself is after me personally. I must escape and find my friends.*

D'Artagnan and Planchet gathered several horses and rode out to the inn where they had left Porthos.

"Oh yes," the innkeeper said, when D'Artagnan arrived. "Monsieur Porthos is here. He is in our best room, in fact. We have been worried about him."

"Is he hurt?" D'Artagnan asked.

"No, we were worried about his expenses," said the innkeeper. "He eats our best food every day, but we haven't been able to get him to pay us. Whenever we ask, he nearly attacks us. Everyone here is terrified of him."

"He does have a short temper," D'Artagnan said, laughing. "Especially when he has no money. You don't need to worry. He will be able to pay you. He's under the protection of a fine, wealthy young lady back in Paris. He has told me this many times."

"I'm afraid he hasn't told you everything, then," the innkeeper said. "You see, he gave us a letter for his duchess and I decided to bring it to her myself. His young lady is actually well over fifty years old, although she behaves as if she's much younger."

"She isn't wealthy or beautiful?" D'Artagnan asked.

"Unfortunately not," said the innkeeper. "She called him nasty names and said she would not help him until he came to see her, even though he was hurt. He was injured in his duel, you see. The man he fought managed to hurt

Monsieur Porthos quite badly. After the duel, the man asked for your friend's name. When he learned it was Porthos, the man apologized and said he had been looking for a Monsieur D'Artagnan. Do you know him?"

"I've never heard of him," D'Artagnan said carefully. "Please tell me where my friend is and I will make sure you are paid for his stay."

The innkeeper directed D'Artagnan to a room upstairs where Porthos and his assistant were playing cards.

"D'Artagnan, is that you?" Porthos said. "It is good to see you again, at last! I'm afraid I can't stand up to greet you, for I'm still injured. Have you spoken to the landlord about me?"

D'Artagnan didn't want to embarrass his friend, so he said the landlord hadn't said anything about him. Porthos told D'Artagnan that he had easily won his fight with the stranger, but then he had tripped over some rocks and hurt himself. D'Artagnan knew his friend was too embarrassed to say that he hadn't won the duel.

"Why haven't you come back to Paris?" he asked.

"I was going to return. I'm very bored here," Porthos said. "Unfortunately, I met some travelers one night and, even though they seemed friendly, they stole my money and my horses while I was asleep. I've been waiting for my beautiful duchess to send me the money to return. She is very much in love with me, you understand. I'm sure she will send the money when she receives my letter."

"I know she will," D'Artagnan said. Then he told Porthos of his adventures since they had last seen each other.

Later that night, D'Artagnan and Planchet left to find Aramis. Before riding away, D'Artagnan made sure to pay the innkeeper for Porthos. He also left behind a horse for Porthos to ride home.

When D'Artagnan and Planchet arrived at the inn where they had left Aramis, they couldn't find him anywhere. They asked around and soon learned that he had been staying with the local priests. He had decided to give up being a Musketeer to become a priest!

"Is this my friend, Aramis?" D'Artagnan asked when he found him at the church. "You look different."

"I have changed my Musketeer's uniform for a priest's cloak," Aramis said with a calm, slightly sad voice. "I feel quite at peace here."

"I was hoping to bring you back with me," D'Artagnan said. "Our adventure isn't over yet. The young woman has been kidnapped again."

"I don't think I'll return. I know you love this young woman, but I must stay here. I no longer have a place in my life for love," Aramis said.

D'Artagnan realized his friend must be heart-broken over someone.

"Perhaps this letter will change your mind," he said. "It arrived for you the day I left Paris. I believe it is scented with a woman's perfume."

Aramis took the letter from him and opened it quickly.

"I thought she had forgotten me," he said, and hugged D'Artagnan. "You see, the woman I love was sent away by the Cardinal. She was trying to help the Queen with a secret plan and the Cardinal found out. I thought I would never see her again."

Then D'Artagnan understood. This was the woman he had seen Madame Bonacieux speaking to the night she visited Aramis's home. This was the same woman who owned the handkerchief that had caused the fight between him and Aramis and him so long ago.

"So you will come back with me?" D'Artagnan asked.

"Of course, my friend," Aramis said.

But the next day when Aramis tried to mount his horse, D'Artagnan saw that his friend was still injured.

"Take care of yourself," D'Artagnan said. "I will look for Athos alone."

He left Aramis with one of the new horses and returned to the inn where he had left Athos fighting for his life.

"Do you recognize me?" D'Artagnan asked the innkeeper who had accused Athos of being a counterfeiter. "A few weeks ago you charged a friend of mine with trying to use fake money."

"Please, Monsieur," the innkeeper said. "I made an awful mistake and I have already paid dearly for it. I was told that there would be criminals traveling through here, and you and your friend matched their descriptions. The Cardinal himself sent soldiers to help me."

"Where is the gentleman?" D'Artagnan asked.

"First let me explain," the innkeeper said. "Your friend fought bravely, for there were seven men attacking him. In the battle, he retreated to the cellar where I store my food. Once inside, he closed the door and locked himself in. When I learned he wasn't a criminal, I tried to tell him that he was safe, but he didn't believe me. He only opened the door once to allow his assistant in. They have been there ever since, eating my food. I'm losing all of my business because of them."

"Then you have the punishment you deserve," D'Artagnan said, and laughed. "You were tricked by the Cardinal."

Suddenly they heard a loud crash. The innkeeper led D'Artagnan to the cellar door.

"I warn you," yelled Athos from the other side of the door, "I will hurt the next person who knocks on that door!"

"I promise, no one will knock without your permission," D'Artagnan said.

"Is that you, my friend?" Athos asked, and opened the door.

When he saw D'Artagnan, he hugged him like a long lost brother.

The innkeeper was shocked when he finally entered the cellar. There was food and broken furniture everywhere. D'Artagnan offered to give the innkeeper Athos's horse to pay for the damages.

"Not to worry," D'Artagnan told Athos. "I have brought a new and far better horse for you."

That night they celebrated being reunited, but then Athos's mood changed. They had been talking about the women Porthos and Aramis loved. D'Artagnan had just started to talk about Madame Bonacieux when Athos interrupted.

"I also have a story to tell you about love. This happened to a friend of mine many years ago," he said.

"Of course," D'Artagnan replied, although he knew that Athos was speaking about himself. He knew the story would be too painful for Athos to tell if he admitted it was his own.

"My friend was a Count in his province. Then he met a young woman who had traveled to his town with her brother. My friend and this woman fell deeply in love and were soon married. One day he learned that she was in fact a thief. The man who said he was her brother was actually her partner in crime! My friend was terribly angry. When he confronted her, she attacked him and tried to kill him! He fought back, but she escaped, taking a precious family heirloom with her. He never saw her again."

"That's a sad story," D'Artagnan said. "I'm sorry for your friend."

CHAPTER 10

Lord de Winter and Lady Clarik

∽

The next morning, D'Artagnan couldn't find their new horses anywhere.

"This is a little embarrassing," Athos said. "You see, after you went to bed I stayed up and talked with some travelers who arrived late. I didn't pay attention, and it seems those men stole our horses. I am sorry, my friend."

And so D'Artagnan and Athos were left to ride their assistants' horses, while those two men walked. Later, when they met up with Aramis and Porthos, they learned that the two

Musketeers had also lost their horses. Porthos had sold his to pay for the extra expenses at the inn, and Aramis had fallen prey to some traveling thieves.

"You are truly great Musketeers," said D'Artagnan, laughing. "And yet none of you can hold on to a good horse."

When the Musketeers arrived in Paris a few days later and reported to Monsieur de Tréville, D'Artagnan learned that he had been granted permission to leave the Cardinal's service and become a Musketeer. He needed to fight only one more battle. At last, his dream would come true! He and his friends celebrated that night.

But their happiness was interrupted with the news that the King planned to send them into battle soon. That meant they would need good horses and equipment. None of them had any money for this, and they stared at each other glumly.

"There is one thing," Athos said at last. "None of you has mentioned that priceless diamond that sparkles whenever D'Artagnan raises his hand."

"This was a gift from the Queen," D'Artagnan said.

But he knew he had no choice. Now that he was to become a Musketeer, he would need equipment for battle. And all four friends had promised to look out for one another.

One day soon after, as D'Artagnan was walking past a church, he saw Porthos speaking quietly to a woman. D'Artagnan realized that this must be the "duchess" Porthos had spoken of so often. The innkeeper had been right. She was not nearly as beautiful or young as Porthos claimed.

Then D'Artagnan realized that sitting near them was the woman he had seen the man from Meung speaking to that first day at the inn, the spy named Milady!

He followed her to her carriage. He knew she

was working with the man from Meung—the man who had kidnapped Madame Bonacieux. Perhaps Milady could lead D'Artagnan to his love. After a journey across the city, the carriage stopped and she leaned out of the window to speak to a man. D'Artagnan rode to the other side of the carriage and looked in. The man she was speaking to saw D'Artagnan and yelled, "It's you!"

"Hello again," D'Artagnan said, surprised.

This was the same man D'Artagnan had fought in Calais. D'Artagnan had stolen his letter of permission in order to take the ship to London.

As soon as Milady saw D'Artagnan, she closed the curtain of her carriage window and told her driver to take her home at once.

"Good-bye, sister," said the man as she drove away.

"And what is your name?" D'Artagnan asked.

"I am Lord de Winter," the man said. "You

attacked me and stole my letter. You shall not defeat me a second time."

"When shall we fight?" D'Artagnan asked.

They agreed on a time and place, and D'Artagnan left to tell his friends. At three o'clock, the four men met with Lord de Winter and his three friends. The groups of men did not like one another and soon all eight men began to duel.

It didn't last very long. Soon only D'Artagnan and Lord de Winter were still fighting. Finally D'Artagnan knocked the sword out of Lord de Winter's hand.

"I could hurt you," D'Artagnan said, thinking of a plan. "But I know you have a sister and I wouldn't want to upset her."

Lord de Winter appreciated D'Artagnan's kindness and invited him to dinner that night. He told D'Artagnan he could meet his sister, whose name was Lady Clarik.

"She is actually my sister-in-law," Lord de Winter said. "She married my brother, the poor lad. He died a few months ago."

When D'Artagnan arrived at Lord de Winter's house, Milady thanked him for not hurting her brother-in-law and D'Artagnan's plan became clearer. He would try to become friends with her and convince her that he loved her. Perhaps then he could learn more about what had happened to Constance.

He returned to visit Milady the next day, and the next, and the next again. Each time she seemed a little friendlier and a little happier to see him.

Slowly, D'Artagnan began to convince Milady that he was in love with her. He went to see her many times, but he was never able to learn any of her secrets. Although Milady wouldn't discuss her work, she did give D'Artagnan one of her favorite pieces of jewelry to show how much she liked him—a gold ring with a large sapphire.

When D'Artagnan described his situation to Athos, his friend grabbed his arm.

"Let me see the ring," Athos said. His face was red with anger and he held D'Artagnan's arm tightly.

"It couldn't be the same," Athos said. "But it is! It's scratched here. I remember this mark. I used to own this ring. My mother gave it to me. Her mother gave it to her. It was meant to be

handed down through the generations of my family."

"And you sold it?" D'Artagnan asked nervously.

"No," Athos said with a strange smile. "I gave it to the woman I loved. Your Milady, or Lady Clarik, or whatever her new name is—she is the same woman I loved. The story I told you was not about my friend. It happened to me. D'Artagnan, you are like a brother to me and I must warn you. Stay away from this woman."

D'Artagnan stopped visiting Milady at once. After a few days, she sent him a letter. She was worried that he had been hurt. D'Artagnan decided to confront her one more time.

"At last, you're here," she said when he entered her room. "I thought I might have scared you away."

"Not exactly," he said. "But you see, I must tell you the truth and I hope you will do the same for me. One of my closest friends, perhaps the closest of all, is someone you know. He recognized the ring you gave me."

Milady sat down. Her skin was pale.

"I know you are a spy for the Cardinal," he said. "I know you are involved in the kidnapping of Constance Bonacieux, the woman I truly love. And I know you are a thief."

D'Artagnan was about to ask her about Constance, but he didn't get the chance. Milady jumped from her chair and ran at him with a dagger. At first he was too surprised to move. Then, treating it as a duel, he sidestepped and avoided her attacks.

"You beast!" she screamed.

D'Artagnan slowly worked his way toward the door. Milady threw furniture over in her efforts to reach him, but D'Artagnan used the furniture to block her way. The door was open just a little. When D'Artagnan got close, he sprang at it and shut the bolts behind him. Milady tried to force the door open. When she couldn't, she stabbed the dagger at the door. D'Artagnan fled down the stairs and into the street.

The next day, he told Athos what had happened.

"You must take extra care, my friend," said Athos. "She is dangerous enough on her own, but the Cardinal is also angry with us."

"Well, now you can have your family heirloom back," said D'Artagnan.

"I want you to sell it," Athos said. "It has bad memories for me. Besides, with the money you get we will have enough for our equipment."

Just then Planchet arrived with two letters. The first gave directions to a deserted part of the city. Beneath the directions was a brief note:

Be in this location at seven o'clock tonight and look carefully into the carriages as they pass. If you care for the woman who loves you, you must say nothing and allow the carriage to pass without trying to follow it. She is risking everything so she can see you for a moment.

Athos and D'Artagnan showed the note to the other Musketeers, who warned D'Artagnan that it might be a trick. D'Artagnan told his friends that he must see Constance, so all four friends decided to go. Athos, Porthos, and Aramis would hide and watch D'Artagnan to make sure nothing happened to him.

Then Athos reminded him of the second letter. D'Artagnan opened it and found an official order to meet with the Cardinal at eight o'clock that night.

"This appointment is more serious than the first," Athos said. "The Cardinal might have some kind of trick in mind for you."

The three Musketeers agreed to wait outside

the Cardinal's palace. If they saw D'Artagnan get arrested, they would fight to free him.

That night, the four men went to the place mentioned in the first letter. Just as night was falling, a carriage appeared, speeding down the road. D'Artagnan felt his heart beating faster. Suddenly a woman's face appeared at the carriage window. She held two fingers to her lips as if telling him to be quiet, or as if sending him a kiss. The carriage passed quickly, but D'Artagnan was sure he had seen Constance!

Even though he had been warned not to follow, D'Artagnan spurred his horse into a gallop. He couldn't catch up to the carriage, though, and was forced to watch it speed away.

CHAPTER 11

Milady Seeks Revenge

∽

When D'Artagnan's friends caught up to him, they all agreed that they had seen Madame Bonacieux at the window of the carriage. Athos said he had also seen a man sitting next to her.

"They must be moving her from one hiding place to another," D'Artagnan said. "The kidnappers still have her. They must have been warning me to stay away."

"At least you know that she is alive," said Athos.

Then Athos reminded D'Artagnan of his

second appointment, and the four men hurried across the city to the Cardinal's palace. As they had planned, Athos, Porthos, and Aramis waited outside.

When D'Artagnan entered the Cardinal's office, the Cardinal was sitting at his desk. He was watching D'Artagnan carefully.

D'Artagnan worked hard to hide his nervousness. The Cardinal seemed to know everything about him: his hometown, his family, his travel to Paris, and his adventure in England.

"On your return from London, you met with a very important person," the Cardinal said. "I see you still wear the jewel that lady gave you."

D'Artagnan tried to hide the ring, but it was too late.

"You are a brave man," the Cardinal said. "But I should warn you that you have powerful enemies. Be careful or they will destroy you.

Now tell me, how would you like a promotion? I'm offering to make you a lieutenant in my guards."

"But all of my friends are in the Musketeers," D'Artagnan said. "It has always been my dream to be a Musketeer, and I am finally close to becoming one."

"Are you refusing me?" the Cardinal asked. "Do you think you're too good to be one of my guards?"

"Not at all," D'Artagnan said, carefully. "But I haven't proven myself in battle yet. It wouldn't feel right to consider your offer until I do that."

"Very well," the Cardinal said. "But remember my offer, and remember that you turned me down."

D'Artagnan met his friends outside and told them what happened. They all congratulated him and told him that he had done the right thing. They agreed to watch out for one another even more carefully from now on. The Cardinal was not to be trusted.

A few days later, the men left for battle. The Duke had kept his word and started a war with France. The first battle was going to take place in the town of La Rochelle. As D'Artagnan rode out of the city, he thought about Constance and about the Cardinal's words. He was so distracted that he failed to notice Milady and two men watching him. She pointed to D'Artagnan and the men nodded and rode after him.

On the way to La Rochelle, D'Artagnan traveled with the Cardinal's guards. During this time, he became separated from the Musketeers. One day as D'Artagnan was walking ahead of the other soldiers, he heard footsteps coming from the forest. He looked around and saw two soldiers running at him with their swords drawn.

D'Artagnan fought the two men and quickly injured one of them. He soon knocked the sword from the other man's hand. He pressed the point of his own sword to the man's chest.

"Speak quickly," D'Artagnan said. "Who hired you to attack me?"

"A woman, monsieur," the man said. "I don't know her name. They call her Milady."

"And what else did she pay you to do?" D'Artagnan asked.

"She hired me and my friend to carry off a young woman and bring her to a convent in Bethune."

Constance, D'Artagnan thought.

D'Artagnan decided not to hurt the young man. Instead, he insisted that the boy tell him the location of the convent. In return, D'Artagnan agreed to protect him from Milady, who would surely seek revenge. The boy told D'Artagnan

that his name was Brisemont and the two headed back to camp.

⌒

A few days later, a letter and a basket of fresh fruit arrived for D'Artagnan. The letter was from Athos. It said that he and the other Musketeers missed D'Artagnan and had decided to send him this basket as a gift. D'Artagnan smiled and decided to save the fruit to share with his friends.

The next day, the Musketeers arrived to surprise D'Artagnan. Their plans had changed, and they met up with D'Artagnan's group sooner than expected. D'Artagnan welcomed his friends and thanked Athos for the fruit.

"But I didn't send you anything," Athos said.

D'Artagnan and the Musketeers hurried back to camp and found Brisemont lying on the ground. He was very sick.

"I ate some of the fruit that was on your table," he said.

"It must have been poisoned!" D'Artagnan said. "Someone faked this letter from Athos and tried to kill me."

"It had to be either Milady or the Cardinal," Athos said. "My friends, we can't go on with so many dangers around us. D'Artagnan must settle this problem with Milady. You must tell her you will tell the King about her past as a thief if she doesn't leave us alone. If the King knows this, he will have her arrested."

"But what of Constance?" D'Artagnan asked. "How do we help her?"

"It's simple," Porthos said. "Brisemont told you where she is being held. Once the battle at La Rochelle is over, we will travel there and rescue her."

CHAPTER 12

Athos Meets His Old Love

A few days later, the three Musketeers were riding back from an inn where they had just eaten dinner. The army was preparing for the battle at La Rochelle and the Musketeers had a few days off before the fight. As they rode, they suddenly heard horses approaching. Athos called out, "Who goes there?"

"Who goes there, yourselves?" one of the riders replied.

"We are Musketeers," Athos said. "Under the command of Monsieur de Tréville."

"Tell me your name," the rider said sharply and rode forward a few steps into the light so the Musketeers could see who was speaking to them.

"Monsieur Cardinal!" Athos said.

"Your name," the Cardinal commanded again.

"Athos."

"I know you," the Cardinal said. "You may not be my friend, but you are brave, loyal, and trustworthy. I would like you and your friends to come on a mission with me tonight. I know I will be safe with you. My mission is secret, but it would be a great favor if you would guard me. It would make the King happy, too."

The Musketeers bowed and agreed to guard the Cardinal and his men. They rode back to the inn, where the Cardinal went upstairs.

While the Musketeers waited and wondered what the Cardinal was up to, Athos drew his friends to an old stove. The stovepipe went up the ceiling and into the room where the Cardinal was having his meeting. By listening to the pipe, the Musketeers could hear what was happening in the room above.

"You are to go to London tonight," the Cardinal said. "Once there, you must go see the Duke. This is very important, Milady."

"Milady!" Athos whispered.

She began to speak and Athos's friends noticed that he flinched at the sound of her voice.

"What shall I tell him?" Milady asked.

"You must convince the Duke to surrender at La Rochelle," the Cardinal said. "Tell him that I will ruin the Queen if he doesn't. Tell him I have evidence against him and the Queen. Tell him that I know everything."

"What should I do if he refuses and continues to threaten France?" she asked.

"He is in love with all the passion of a madman," the Cardinal said. "Or the passion of a fool. If he believes the Queen is in danger, he will think twice. If he still doesn't change his mind, then perhaps you can see to it that he is injured and unable to continue his plans of attack."

"I understand," Milady said. "Now that I have your instructions about how to deal with your enemies, may I speak to you about mine?"

"Your enemies?" the Cardinal asked.

"I have many," Milady said. "And I have made them all while working for you. But two of them are especially painful to me, and I want your help in punishing them. First, a woman named Constance Bonacieux."

"I know her," the Cardinal said. "You have her held in a convent, do you not? I know she is involved in this business with the Duke. What will you do with her?"

"I will have her moved. I want your men to send her to prison," said Milady. "But it is my other enemy that I truly need your help with. He is even worse than Madame Bonacieux. He is the man who loves her—the scoundrel, D'Artagnan."

"I know him well," the Cardinal said. "He is a bold fellow."

"He is a danger to us all," Milady replied.

"If you can give me proof of his involvement with the Duke, I will have him sent to prison."

"Perfect," Milady said. "Although I was hoping for a bit more. My plans—"

"I don't know what you mean," the Cardinal interrupted. "And I don't want to know. I will write you a note that will allow you to seek your revenge on D'Artagnan. With this, you won't need me."

Athos led his friends away from the stove.

"I must go now," he said. "If the Cardinal asks where I am, tell him I've gone ahead to be a look-out in case the road is unsafe."

"Be careful," Aramis said.

Athos rode a short distance into the woods. Then he turned and hid among the trees to watch the inn. After a few minutes, he saw the Cardinal leave with his men. Aramis and Porthos followed behind them. Athos waited a while longer and then returned to the inn. He went straight to the room where the Cardinal had met with Milady. She was still there.

Athos pulled his hat low so she couldn't see his face clearly.

"Who are you?" she cried when he entered the room.

"It is you, after all," he said. Athos stepped forward and lifted his hat so she could see him. "Do you recognize me, Madame?"

She stepped backward, terrified, as if she had seen a ghost.

"So you do recognize me," Athos said. "You thought I was dead, didn't you? I thought the same of you. After so many years, we find ourselves in a strange position, don't we?"

"Tell me," she said in a faint voice. "Why are you here? What do you want from me?"

"First, I want you to understand that I know everything you have been plotting with the Cardinal," Athos said. "I know of your plans to hurt my friend D'Artagnan and to hurt the Duke of Buckingham."

Athos stepped closer and put his hand on the grip of his sword.

"I swear to you, if D'Artagnan is harmed in any way, I will reveal your secrets to everyone. Then I will come after you myself. Does the Cardinal know you are an escaped thief? What about the King? I'm sure he would like to see you returned to prison."

Athos demanded that Milady give him the letter the Cardinal had just written for her. He read it quickly.

The holder of this letter has been working for me and is to be excused of any crimes.

Cardinal Richelieu.

CHAPTER 13

An Unusual Place for a Meeting

∽

Athos rode back to camp. The other Musketeers were waiting for him. He sent an invitation for D'Artagnan to meet them for breakfast the next day. Then he told Aramis and Porthos that he would tell them everything when all four men were together.

The next day, the four friends tried to find a safe place to discuss the Cardinal and Milady.

"We don't know who might be listening," Athos said. "The Cardinal and Milady have spies everywhere."

While they ate breakfast at an inn full of soldiers, D'Artagnan told his friends that his troop had just seen a small battle at a place called the Bastion Saint-Gervais. One of the soldiers nearby interrupted and said he had heard about it.

"There will be a group going there later today to clean up," he said. "It's a mess after the battle."

"I believe we could make a game of that," Athos said.

"Of what?" the soldier replied.

Several other soldiers turned to listen.

"I believe my friends and I will have lunch at the Bastion Saint-Gervais," Athos said. "We will stay there for one hour and no one will force us to move."

"But the enemy soldiers are still close," the other soldier said. "They are closer to the Bastion than we are. They would attack before you even arrived."

D'Artagnan looked worried, but Athos whispered to him, "This will be the perfect place for our meeting. We can be sure that no one will spy on us there."

The Bastion Saint-Gervais was a small fort between the two army camps. After the previous day's battle, the place was in ruins. Weapons were left on the ground where soldiers had fallen and the walls were crumbling. The Musketeers and their assistants gathered as many weapons as they could, climbed to the highest point of the fort, and set up a picnic lunch.

While their assistants kept a lookout for enemy soldiers, Athos told his friends about his visit with Milady the night before. D'Artagnan almost dropped his glass when he heard the news.

"It seems our friend D'Artagnan is now her biggest enemy," Athos said. "She wishes to do him some harm and the Cardinal has agreed to help her."

"In that case, I am lost," D'Artagnan said. "How can I fight both of them?"

"Don't forget that we're your friends and that we will help you," Athos said calmly.

Grimaud signaled that a troop of enemy soldiers was approaching. The Musketeers quickly set themselves up along the high wall. When the enemy saw them, each side began to fire. The battle was short, and the Musketeers were able to force the enemy soldiers back.

"Now, where were we?" Athos asked after the fight.

"We were discussing Milady," D'Artagnan said.

Athos showed his friends the letter the Cardinal had given to Milady.

"Why, this gives permission for the letter's owner to do anything at all," D'Artagnan said. "It is very powerful. This gives me an idea."

But before he could continue, Grimaud shouted, "To arms, gentlemen!"

Another troop of enemy soldiers was approaching the bastion.

"Perhaps we should make our way back to camp," Porthos said. "We are greatly outnumbered."

"Unfortunately, that is impossible for three reasons," Athos said. "First, we haven't finished eating lunch yet. Second, we still have important business to discuss. And third, we haven't been here for a full hour yet."

So the Musketeers set themselves up as before and, after another short battle, managed to force the enemy troops to retreat. Afterward, the assistants worked together to gather old bits of armor and weapons, which they stood against the wall to make it look as if there were several soldiers standing guard.

"Perhaps this will make them think twice before attacking again," Aramis said. "They'll think we have more soldiers with us than we really do. Now, D'Artagnan, what was your idea?"

"We must warn the Queen and the Duke," D'Artagnan began. "I could return to London—"

"No, none of us can leave camp now," Athos interrupted. "The Cardinal and Milady will be watching all of us closely."

Suddenly the Musketeers heard gunfire in the distance. The enemy soldiers were approaching again, this time with a much larger force.

"My friends," Athos said, "I believe we have been here long enough to win our game. It is time for us to return."

The men hurried back to camp. Every soldier was waiting and watching for them. There was a large crowd—over two thousand soldiers—and they all burst into cheers when the Musketeers returned. News of their adventure spread quickly.

An amazing feat, the Cardinal thought when he

heard the news. *I must try to get those men on my side. Perhaps I can do them a favor.*

The Cardinal spoke to Monsieur de Tréville to congratulate him on his brave soldiers.

"But D'Artagnan is not one of mine, sir," Monsieur de Tréville said. "He is still a member of the Royal Guards."

"Then take him," the Cardinal said. "He's always with his friends in the Musketeers. It's time he was made one of them."

CHAPTER 14

Lord de Winter's Revenge

⌐𝕆⌐

"At last!" D'Artagnan cried when he learned the news. "Thank you, Athos. It was a great idea to meet at the Bastion Saint-Gervais. The Cardinal even seems to like us more for the bravery we showed there. And I've come up with an idea for warning the Duke and the Queen. We will write letters to each of them."

"I believe we should write to Lord de Winter, instead of the Duke," Aramis said. "With the Cardinal's spies everywhere, we would never be able to get a letter to the Duke. And Lord de Winter may be able to stop Milady."

The others agreed, and Aramis began to compose a letter.

"If I am to warn Lord de Winter about his sister-in-law, I will need more information about her," he said. "What else do you know about Milady?"

D'Artagnan looked at Athos, who thought for a while before finally telling the others about her.

"She is a thief," he said. "She escaped from prison and married Lord de Winter's brother, who died shortly afterward. It is likely that she killed him to inherit his fortune."

"How did you learn this?" Porthos asked.

"I knew her before she met Lord de Winter's brother," Athos said. "She was my wife. When I discovered her secret, she tried to kill me."

"It seems we Musketeers are not so lucky in love," Porthos said, and laughed bitterly.

"How do we warn the Queen?" Athos asked. "If we go to her, the Cardinal will surely see us."

"I can help," Aramis said. "The woman I love is one of the Queen's seamstresses. She has helped us in the past. The last time the Duke was in Paris, in fact."

So Aramis wrote one letter to Lord de Winter, and one to his love, asking her to warn the Queen. The Musketeers sent Planchet to London with the letter for Lord de Winter, and asked Bazin to deliver the letter to the seamstress.

Meanwhile, Milady was on a ship headed for London. She was furious with D'Artagnan for insulting her and with Athos for threatening her. She was anxious to complete her mission in London so she could return to France and take revenge.

After several days, her ship approached

London's harbor. Before they landed, a smaller boat came out to meet them. A young man dressed in a naval officer's uniform boarded the ship and asked Milady to come with him.

"But I'm Lady Clarik," Milady said with a perfect English accent. "Lord de Winter is my brother-in-law."

"I'm sorry," the young officer said. "You must come with me. Those are my orders."

When they reached the shore, the young officer took her to a castle far from London. He walked her to the tower and led her to a small room with a heavy door that locked from the outside.

"I see I am a prisoner," Milady said. "Is this to be my cell?"

"Please stay here," the officer said. "Someone will explain everything soon."

Milady was even angrier than before. *The Musketeers must have warned the Duke of Buckingham,* she thought. After a short time in her cell, Milady heard the door open and Lord de Winter entered.

"Hello, sister-in-law," he said. "Welcome to my castle."

"You!" she said. "Then I am your prisoner? What is this about?"

"You've decided to return to England," he said, ignoring her question.

"I came to see you," Milady said.

"What's wrong with wanting to see my brother-in-law?"

"Come, Milady," Lord de Winter said. "I know your secret. I received a letter from the Musketeers. I believe you know them. One of them used to be your husband. I know you and the Cardinal have some mischief in mind for the Duke of Buckingham. Well, none of that will happen. You will stay here for a time and then I shall have you sent far away. If you ever return to England, I will make sure you are sent back to prison."

Lord de Winter left and Milady sat next to the window watching the sea. She tried to think of a way to escape.

After a few days in her cell, Milady learned that the young officer who had brought her to the castle was named Felton. He came to see her several times a day, to deliver food and ask if she needed anything. This gave Milady an idea. She knew men found her beautiful. Perhaps she could use that beauty to make the young man fall in love with her.

⤳

It took several days for Milady's plan to work. She studied Felton, pretended to be different than she really was, and watched how he behaved around her. She learned how to make him feel sorry for her and how to make him believe her when she told a lie.

One day Milady discovered that Lord de Winter hadn't told Felton why she was being held prisoner. Trying to sway him to her side, she told the young man she was innocent and that Lord de Winter and the Duke of Buckingham were working together.

"They have a plan to hurt the King of England," she said. "I discovered their secret and that's why my evil brother-in-law put me here."

At first Felton didn't believe her, but she acted so innocently and Lord de Winter hated her so much that he began to change his mind. Lord de Winter noticed that something about Felton had changed and ordered him to go on a mission to another city. On the day Felton was to leave, Milady heard a tap at her window.

"Felton," she cried when she opened the window. "I am saved!"

"I will set you free," said Felton. "Hush! I need time to saw the bars. You must make sure no one sees me if they come to your door."

Hours later, Felton tapped at the window again. He had made a small opening by removing two of the iron bars.

When Felton and Milady were free of her cell, he brought her to the seaside. A small boat and crew were waiting for her.

"This boat will take you anywhere you want to go, my love," said Felton. "I must return to London."

"But why?" Milady asked.

"I must stop the Duke," Felton replied. "He cannot be allowed to hurt the King."

Milady was pleased. Not only would she be free to seek revenge on the Musketeers, but this young man was going to accomplish her mission for her.

The next day, Felton raced to the Duke's mansion. He knocked on the door and said that he had an important message to deliver. When the Duke entered the room, Felton attacked and wounded him terribly.

Felton was immediately arrested and a doctor was sent to help the Duke. The doctor said the Duke would recover, but he was hurt too badly to go to the battle at La Rochelle. This meant he wouldn't be able to see his love, the Queen of France. His plans were ruined.

Meanwhile, Milady arrived in France and traveled to the convent where she had hidden Constance Bonacieux. Milady had never seen Madame Bonacieux and wasn't sure who she was.

Milady pretended to be a prisoner of the Cardinal. She began talking to the other women and tried to learn which of them was Constance. But everyone was suspicious of her questions. Milady had to work hard to earn the trust of the other women.

When she finally found Constance, Milady pretended to be her friend. One day, as the two women were sitting together, Milady asked Constance about her love.

"There is a young man named D'Artagnan," Constance said. "He will come to rescue me. I know he will."

Milady and Constance waited and watched everyone who approached. After a few days, a rider came galloping toward the convent. Milady worried that it might be D'Artagnan. When she looked closer, she was happy to see that it was actually Count Rochefort—D'Artagnan's man from Meung.

Milady met with the Count in private and learned that the Musketeers would soon be on their way. With the Duke injured, there would be no battle at La Rochelle. The King was bringing his soldiers back to Paris.

Milady told Rochefort to meet her in a town called Armentières in a few days. She would bring Constance there.

After Rochefort left, Milady returned to Constance and began to lie to her. Milady said she had just met with her brother. He had told her that the Cardinal's guards were on their way to bring Milady and Constance to prison.

"What's worse, D'Artagnan and his Musketeers are delayed at La Rochelle," Milady said. "My brother has heard horrible reports of the battle there. It appears no one will be coming to rescue you."

"What shall we do?" Constance asked.

"I told my brother to send a carriage," said Milady. "He will meet me in a town called Armentières. You could come with me. Then we can both escape the Cardinal."

"But what if D'Artagnan does come for me?" asked Constance.

"He won't, dear," said Milady. "The battle at La Rochelle is still going on. He will be there for many days."

Milady knew that D'Artagnan could arrive at any moment. She wanted to leave with Constance as soon as the carriage arrived.

Meanwhile, the Musketeers arrived back in Paris and asked Monsieur de Tréville for permission to take a few days away. Monsieur de Tréville agreed, and the men left to rescue Constance.

That night, they stopped at an inn for dinner. When D'Artagnan stepped outside, he saw a man get on a horse and gallop away, back toward Paris. It was the man from Meung!

"That's the man!" D'Artagnan cried. "My enemy! Let me catch up to him."

Athos said they should all go after him, but Aramis disagreed.

"Not now, my friends," he said. "That man is going back to Paris. We are on a mission to rescue Constance Bonacieux from a convent in Bethune. We must save her first."

CHAPTER 15

The End of Milady's Plan

That evening, Milady and Constance heard horses galloping on the road. Milady rushed to the window and was relieved to see her carriage outside. She told Constance they had to leave now, before the Cardinal's guards came for them.

"I don't know what to do," Constance said. "I can barely move. I still believe D'Artagnan will come for me."

"There's no time," Milady said.

Just then, she heard more horses on the road and saw D'Artagnan in the distance!

Milady was terrified. She took a glass of water and secretly dropped a small red pill into it. Then she gave the glass to Constance. Milady wanted her revenge on D'Artagnan, one way or another.

"Here, drink this," Milady said. "It will help you relax. Then we must be going."

As soon as Constance drank it, she began to feel strange. A wave of dizziness passed over her and she fell to the floor. When she woke up, she was lying on the ground and D'Artagnan was holding her hand.

"Constance, are you all right?" he asked.

"I feel so sick," she said weakly. "Is that you, D'Artagnan? I knew you would come to rescue me."

Aramis picked up the water glass and examined it. He sniffed it carefully and scraped out some of the powder that had settled at the bottom.

"Did you drink from this?" he asked.

"Yes, she gave it to me," Constance said. "Is she here? She wanted to help me."

"Who?" Athos asked.

"Lady Clarik," Constance said. "She's another prisoner here. She was very kind to me. She wanted to take me to Armentières."

The Musketeers looked at each other and knew at once that Milady had tried to poison her. The matter was grim, but no one wanted to upset Constance. Instead, they helped her to bed. She was very sick.

Suddenly the Musketeers heard a horse galloping toward the convent. When they ran outside, they saw that Lord de Winter had arrived.

"I'm surprised to see you here," he said. "I've come to find Lady Clarik. I was holding her prisoner, but she escaped before I could send her away. She tricked one of my soldiers into helping her. My soldier, the poor fool, attacked the Duke and injured him badly."

"We'll find her together," Athos said. "We all have reason to be angry with her, although I believe she injured me first."

Leaving Constance in the care of the nuns at the convent, the four Musketeers and Lord de Winter rode to the town of Armentières. On the way, they passed a small port where there were a few boats docked. Athos left the group for a short time to talk to some of the men at the docks. He came back with a mysterious man, who didn't say anything to the others. The group rode toward the inn to capture Milady, each man deep in his own dark thoughts.

The six men approached the inn quietly and looked in the window. They saw Milady sitting alone at a table. The lightning flashed and she saw Athos staring at her through the window. Then D'Artagnan kicked the door open. The four Musketeers and Lord de Winter entered the room.

"What do you want?" she cried.

"We want to judge you for your crimes," Athos said. "D'Artagnan, you first."

"I accuse you of trying to kill me and my friends," D'Artagnan said. "Worst of all, you kidnapped and poisoned my love, Constance Bonacieux."

Then Lord de Winter stepped forward.

"I accuse you of causing the attack on the Duke of Buckingham," he said.

"It is now my turn," Athos said. "I accuse you of lying to me, marrying me as someone else, and then trying to kill me when I discovered the truth."

The mysterious man from the docks entered the room and Athos pointed at Milady. The man took her and tied her arms behind her back. Then he blindfolded her.

"Our friend here will take you to his boat," Athos said. "He will make sure you are sent far from here. You will be at sea for a long time. Do not try to return to France or England again. Be thankful you are leaving with your life."

⟡

Back in Paris, the four Musketeers were having dinner when the man from Meung interrupted them.

"We meet at last," D'Artagnan said, drawing his sword. "This time you shall not escape me."

"I don't wish to escape," the man said. "In fact, I have come for you. In the name of the King and the Cardinal, I am placing you under arrest. I must ask that you come with me right now. Your life is at stake."

"Who are you?" D'Artagnan asked.

"My name is Rochefort," he said. "I am an agent of the Cardinal. I have orders to bring you to him now."

D'Artagnan looked at his friends. He knew

they would fight for him, but he wanted to end his problems with the Cardinal once and for all.

"Very well," D'Artagnan said. "I will go with you. But my friends are coming, too. They will wait for me outside the Cardinal's office."

"The Cardinal expected that," Rochefort said. "He will be pleased."

When D'Artagnan entered his office, the Cardinal was sitting at his desk. D'Artagnan bowed and sat in the chair facing him.

"You are being charged with a great many crimes," the Cardinal said. "You have helped the Duke of Buckingham, and you have been working to ruin my plans. In short, you are a traitor."

"Who has accused me?" D'Artagnan asked. "Was it a woman named Lady Clarik? Perhaps you know her as Milady. That woman is a murderer and an escaped thief."

"If she is, you can be sure she will be punished," the Cardinal said.

"She has already been punished," D'Artagnan said. "She has been sent away, never to return to France or England. I have made sure of it."

"You have no right to make such decisions!" said the Cardinal. "You are not a judge and can be punished for acting as one."

"I know," D'Artagnan said. "And I will accept your decision."

"You are a brave man," the Cardinal said. "Do you know that I can have you tried and found guilty?"

"I understand," said D'Artagnan. "But you must understand something, too. If you try to punish me, I will be pardoned."

"Pardoned?" the Cardinal asked. "Who would pardon your crime—the King?"

"No, sir," said D'Artagnan. "I have already been pardoned by you."

"You have lost your mind," the Cardinal said.

"Surely you will recognize your own handwriting?" D'Artagnan asked, handing over the letter that Athos had taken from Milady:

The holder of this letter has been working for me and is to be excused of any crimes.

Cardinal Richelieu.

The Cardinal read the letter carefully, then stared at D'Artagnan for a long time.

He's certainly an extraordinary young man, the Cardinal thought. *And Milady was a dangerous person to have on my side. Perhaps it is better that she is gone, after all.*

The Cardinal was lost in his thoughts. He rolled and unrolled the paper in his hands. Then he looked at D'Artagnan and saw all the suffering the young man had endured in his adventures. The Cardinal thought D'Artagnan had a bright future ahead of him. The boy's courage and intelligence would be good to have on his side.

Slowly, the Cardinal tore up the letter.

This is the end, D'Artagnan thought, and he bowed to the Cardinal.

The Cardinal took out another piece of paper and wrote a short note, which he handed to D'Artagnan.

"I have taken from you a letter which gave the holder a great gift," the Cardinal said. "The King has given me permission to give you another gift. There is no name on this letter. You may write it in on your own."

D'Artagnan read the new letter. It was a promotion! If D'Artagnan wrote his name on it, he would become a Lieutenant in the Musketeers. He fell to one knee.

"Sir, my life is yours," D'Artagnan said. "I don't deserve this favor from you. I have three friends who are all more deserving—"

"You are a brave and generous lad," the Cardinal interrupted. "Do with the letter what you wish. But remember, I gave it to *you*. I wish for *you* to have the promotion."

D'Artagnan returned to his friends and showed them the letter. He offered it to each of them, but they all refused.

"No one deserves it more than you," Athos said.

Then he took the letter and wrote on it "D'Artagnan."

What Do *You* Think?
Questions for Discussion

⌒

Have you ever been around a toddler who keeps asking the question "Why?" Does your teacher call on you in class with questions from your homework? Do your parents ask you questions about your day at the dinner table? We are always surrounded by questions that need a specific response. But is it possible to have a question with no right answer?

The following questions are about the book you just read. But this is not a quiz! They are designed to help you look at the people, places, and events in the story from different angles. These questions do not have specific answers. Instead, they might make you think of the story in a completely new way.

Think carefully about each question and enjoy discovering more about this classic story.

1. The Musketeers' motto is "All for one and one for all." What do you think this means? Do you have any friends that are this loyal to you? Is there anyone to whom you are this loyal?

2. Porthos tells Aramis that he must be either a priest or a Musketeer, but not both. Why do you suppose Aramis can't be both? Which do you think he would be better at? What do you want to be when you grow up?

3. When the King gives D'Artagnan money, the Musketeers tell him to get an assistant. What qualities would you look for in an assistant? Would you ever want to be an assistant to a Musketeer?

4. Why do you think Athos decides to go to jail for D'Artagnan? Have you ever lied to protect a friend? What's the biggest lie you've ever told?

5. When D'Artagnan tells Monsieur de Tréville that he has a secret, Monsieur de Tréville asks if it is his secret to share. Has anyone ever asked you to keep a secret for them? Were you able to keep yourself from telling? What's the biggest secret you've ever kept?

6. Why do you think Milady hates D'Artagnan so much? Have you ever had an enemy?

7. Why do you suppose Porthos lied about his lady and how he was injured? Have you ever been too embarrassed to tell the truth? What happened?

8. Do you think the Musketeers were right to send Milady away? Should they have let the King or the Cardinal take care of her instead? What would you have done in their place?

9. Were you surprised that D'Artagnan wrote his own name on the promotion? Would you have done the same? Who do you think was the most deserving of the promotion?

10. Each of the Musketeers is very different from the others. Do you know anyone like these men? Which Musketeer are you the most like?

Afterword
by Arthur Pober, Ed.D.

ᴄᴑ

First impressions are important.

Whether we are meeting new people, going to new places, or picking up a book unknown to us, first impressions count for a lot. They can lead to warm, lasting memories or can make us shy away from any future encounters.

Can you recall your own first impressions and earliest memories of reading the classics?

Do you remember wading through pages and pages of text to prepare for an exam? Or were you the child who hid under the blanket to read with a flashlight, joining forces with Robin Hood to save Maid Marian? Do you remember only how long it took you to read a lengthy novel such as *Little Women*? Or did you become best friends with the March sisters?

Even for a gifted young reader, getting through long chapters with dense language can easily become overwhelming and can obscure the richness of the story and its characters. Reading an abridged, newly crafted version of a classic novel can be the gentle introduction a child needs to explore the characters and storyline without the frustration of difficult vocabulary and complex themes.

Reading an abridged version of a classic novel gives the young reader a sense of independence and the satisfaction of finishing a "grown-up" book. And when a child is engaged with and inspired by a classic story, the tone is set for further exploration of the story's themes, characters, history, and details. As a child's reading skills advance, the desire to tackle the original, unabridged version of the story will naturally emerge.

If made accessible to young readers, these stories can become invaluable tools for understanding themselves in the context of their families and social environments. This is why the Classic Starts series includes questions that stimulate discussion regarding the impact and social relevance of the characters and stories today. These questions can foster lively conversations between children and their parents or teachers. When we look at the issues, values, and standards of past times in terms of how we live now, we can appreciate literature's classic tales in a very personal and engaging way.

Share your love of reading the classics with a young child, and introduce an imaginary world real enough to last a lifetime.

Dr. Arthur Pober, Ed.D.

Dr. Arthur Pober has spent more than twenty years in the fields of early childhood and gifted education. He is the former principal of one of the world's oldest laboratory schools for gifted youngsters, Hunter College Elementary School, and former Director of Magnet Schools for the Gifted and Talented for more than 25,000 youngsters in New York City.

Dr. Pober is a recognized authority in the areas of media and child protection and is currently the U.S. representative to the European Institute for the Media and European Advertising Standards Alliance.

Explore these wonderful stories in our
Classic Starts™ library.

20,000 Leagues Under the Sea

The Adventures of Huckleberry Finn

The Adventures of Robin Hood

The Adventures of Sherlock Holmes

The Adventures of Tom Sawyer

Anne of Green Gables

Around the World in 80 Days

Black Beauty

The Call of the Wild

Dracula

Frankenstein

Gulliver's Travels

Heidi

A Little Princess

Little Women

Oliver Twist

Pollyanna

The Prince and the Pauper

Rebecca of Sunnybrook Farm

The Red Badge of Courage

Robinson Crusoe

The Secret Garden

The Story of King Arthur and His Knights

The Strange Case of Dr. Jekyll and Mr. Hyde

The Swiss Family Robinson

The Three Musketeers

Treasure Island

The War of the Worlds

White Fang

The Wind in the Willows